The Binoculars in the Window Mystery

Elaine Pageler

High Noon Books
Novato, California

Cover Design and Interior Illustrations: Tina Cash

International Standard Book Number: 1-57128-066-9

7 6 5 4 3 2 1 0 9 8
1 0 9 8 7 6 5 4 3 2

Contents

CHAPTER 1

The Windows

Brad Jones hurried to work. He and Meg Green were moving. Their desks had been in the back of the newsroom for a year. Now they would be up front by the window. One of the newsmen had quit. Their boss had given them his space.

Meg was already at work. Her desk drawers had been stacked on the floor. So were lots of file folders.

"We have to work fast. The movie star Denton Bay will be at the Palace Theater in two hours," she said.

Brad started to work. He knew Denton Bay was meeting with the press. The News wanted Brad to take pictures. Meg would write the story about the play at the Palace starring the famous movie star.

It took an hour to move their things. Now they had to be put away.

Meg sat down. She glanced out the window. "This is a great view of Riddle Street. We can see most of the street from here," she said.

Brad looked out, too. An apartment house and a clothing store were on the other side of the street. This side had four buildings. The News was on one end of the block. The Palace

Theater was on the other. Carl's Coffee Shop and the Star Bank were in between.

The smell of coffee drifted up to Brad. It came from Carl's Coffee Shop down below. Brad took a deep breath. Then he went back to work.

"I wish those flashes of light would stop. They shine in my eyes," Meg said.

Brad looked up. "What flashes?" he asked.

Meg pointed to the apartment house across the street. "Look at that window. It's on the fourth floor. The flashes come from there."

Just then Brad saw the flash. He leaned forward and peered out. Someone sat in that window. But Brad couldn't see what the person was doing.

His camera had a long lens. It made things look closer. Brad reached for it and aimed at the window.

"A woman is there. She is looking through a pair of binoculars. The sun strikes the glass. That's why you see flashes," he said.

Meg looked through his camera. "She has a big camera, too. It's on a stand near her," she told him.

Brad took his camera once more. He stared through it. "Look at the size of that lens. She can snap a close-up of anyone on the street. That woman is set up to take pictures. Now she is watching the street. She's waiting for someone," he said.

"The woman could be waiting for Denton Bay. Maybe she's from a magazine. They want her to take pictures of him," Meg said.

Brad nodded. "Sure, she just rents an apartment. It's near the Palace. Then she doesn't have to stand in the crowd," he said.

Meg pointed to the street. "But you do. Here's a TV truck now. The crowd will form soon. Come on. Let's go," she said.

Brad took one last look at the window. The woman was still there. Wait! What was that? Did something move behind her? Was someone else in that room?

But nothing moved again. So Brad turned and followed Meg to the street.

CHAPTER 2

The Actor and the Banker

Brad and Meg went up Riddle Street. The door of Carl's Coffee Shop stood open. Now the smell of coffee was very strong.

"Let's stop and get a cup. We can watch for Denton Bay," Brad said.

"All right," Meg said.

Carl's Coffee Shop was small. It only had a counter. Carl stood behind it. A cabdriver sat on one of the stools. The name Al was written on his shirt. Brad and Meg sat down beside him.

"Two cups of coffee?" Carl asked.

"Yes, it smells good," Brad said.

Meg watched out the window. "Here comes Denton Bay's limo," she said.

The cabdriver shook his head. "Denton Bay has a white limo. This one is black. It belongs to Casper Lloyd," he told them.

Carl put two cups in front of Brad and Meg. "Al's right. Casper Lloyd is the new owner of Star Bank. Riddle Street is doing well. We have a famous actor in our play. Also, we have one of the richest men for our banker," he said.

They watched the limo. It stopped in front of the bank. The driver went around and opened the back door. A short man in a black suit climbed out. He had a briefcase.

The cabdriver grinned. "Look at what that driver has to wear. That guy looks like a toy soldier," he said.

A tall man walked through the door. Brad and Meg knew him. His name was Walt Conner. He used to work for the News. They had just moved to his old space.

"Hi, Walt. I thought you moved out of your apartment. Aren't you leaving town?" Brad asked.

"I'm staying at a hotel for a few days. Denton Bay is here. I'm a big fan," he said.

"He's meeting the press this morning. Are you going?" Meg asked.

"Yes, I kept my press pass. That way I could see the great man," Walt said.

"Are you going to the play?" Brad asked.

"Yes, I have tickets for every night. So what if it's the same play? I like to see him act," he said.

"It's on Friday afternoon, too," Carl said.

"I didn't know that," Walt told him.

Brad tossed some money on the counter. "Carl, the coffee is great. But Denton Bay should be here soon," he said.

"Wait for me," Meg told him.

Walt gulped his coffee. "I'm coming, too," he said.

A group of people were in front of the

A group of people were in front
of the Palace Theater.

Palace Theater. Some had cameras. Others had notebooks. They went inside.

The white limo came down the street. Brad glanced at the window. The woman stood at the camera now. But it wasn't aimed at the Palace. She took pictures of the Star Bank. Brad snapped two pictures. One was of the woman. The other was what she aimed at.

Then Brad turned back to the limo. It had stopped. Denton Bay got out. He wore a hat, dark glasses, and a long coat.

Brad took pictures. Then he went inside. Denton Bay came on stage. He took off his coat, hat, and glasses. Everyone clapped but Walt clapped the loudest.

People asked questions. Walt stood up. "How tall are you, Mr. Bay?" he asked.

Denton Bay looked at him. "I'm 6 foot 4. That must be about your height," he said.

Walt smiled. He sat down.

There were a few more questions. But Brad went outside. He wanted a picture of the actor as he left.

The doors swung open. Denton Bay came out in his hat and coat. The crowd followed.

Brad snapped pictures until the limo left. Then he looked up at the window. Now the woman's binoculars were on the Palace. She was waving at someone in the crowd. Brad wondered who that could be.

CHAPTER 3

Pictures

Brad spent most of the afternoon in the photo lab. Now he picked up the pictures and rushed back to the newsroom.

Meg sat at her desk. She held a pair of binoculars.

"I went out and bought them. The woman still sits in the window. She hasn't taken pictures. But she wouldn't. Denton Bay won't be back until tomorrow night. That's the first play," she said.

Brad shook his head. "Something else is going on. I don't think she took pictures of Denton Bay," he told her.

"Then what's she doing?" Meg asked.

"I don't know. But here are two pictures. The first one is of her. She's taking a picture. The second one is what she aimed at," Brad said.

He showed her the second picture. The black limo was parked in front of the Star Bank. The limo driver stood near it.

Meg frowned. "Why would she take a picture of him?" she asked.

Brad shook his head. He told her about the woman waving.

"She must have a friend," Meg said.

Brad nodded. "I thought someone was in her apartment," he told her.

"I wonder who she and her friend are. And what is she doing?" Meg wanted to know.

Brad showed her something else. "I made the first picture bigger. Look at her face. Have you seen her before?" he asked.

Meg shook her head. "She must be new. That's a nice flowered dress," she said.

"Maybe she's from the police. Denton Bay is famous. Casper Lloyd is rich. They're here in the same block. The police might have a stakeout to keep them safe," Brad said.

"That could be," Meg told them.

Brad reached for the phone and dialed the police. "Is Sergeant Ward there?" he asked.

"Sergeant Ward is out of town. He'll be back in a few days," the voice said.

Brad hung up the phone. "Let's do our story on Denton Bay," he said.

They went to work. Meg typed her story. Brad laid out the pictures. Now it was ready for tomorrow's paper.

Meg leaned back and looked out the window. She jumped up. "The woman's gone!" she gasped.

Brad's head shot up. He didn't need his camera to see. The window was closed and the curtain pulled. Then Brad saw something else.

Casper Lloyd's black limo was gone, too.

"There she is! That's her dress," Meg said. She pointed to a woman coming out of the apartment house.

Brad grabbed his camera case and began to run. He raced down the steps and out the door. The woman wasn't in front of the bank or the Palace. Then he saw her. She was going the other way. He tailed her for two blocks. Then she turned into a camera store. Brad went in, too.

The woman handed the man a film. "When will they be done?" she asked.

"They'll be done by tomorrow morning," he told her. Then he turned to Brad. "Do you have a film, too?" he asked.

Brad had to think fast. He pulled a film from his case. It was one he took last week. He hadn't had time to do it at the News lab.

The man handed him an envelope. Brad wrote "B. Jones." He slipped the film inside.

The woman had gone now. She must have gone back to her apartment. It was late. And Brad had done his work. So he went home.

He picked up the pictures the next morning. It was on his way to work.

Meg spotted them when he walked in. "Are those more pictures of Denton Bay?" she asked.

Brad tossed them to her. "No, they aren't. I took these pictures last week," he told her.

Meg pulled out the pictures. She frowned. "Why did you take pictures of limo drivers?" she asked.

Brad looked over her shoulder. "Those aren't mine," he said.

Meg picked up the envelope. "It says Bea Jones," she told him.

Brad laughed. "I told the man B. Jones. He made a mistake and gave me these," he said.

Meg sorted through the pictures. "Brad, look at these. They're all pictures of the same limo driver. There are front and back and side views. The black limo belongs to Casper Lloyd. I know who owns the pictures. It's the woman in the window," she said.

CHAPTER 4

Following the Woman

Brad and Meg worked fast. They made copies of the pictures. Meg put them back in the envelope. Then Brad rushed them back to the camera store. He got his real pictures and left.

The woman came toward him. Brad got a good look as she walked past. Her eyes were narrowed and her teeth clenched. There was no doubt that she was in a hurry.

Meg waited in front of the News. She had a smile on her face.

"I checked the woman out while you were gone. The apartment on the corner of the fourth floor is 417. And the name on the mailbox is Bea Jones. So we were right," she said.

"Now we need another answer. Why did she take all those pictures of the limo driver?" Brad asked.

Meg looked down the street. "Here Bea comes now," she said.

They thought Bea would go to her rooms. But she stepped to the curb and waved.

"She's hailing a cab. That driver was in Carl's yesterday. I had never seen him before," Brad said.

"His name was Al," Meg told him.

Brad had an idea. "Let's see where she's going. Hurry! My car is in the parking lot," Brad told her.

They raced to his car. Brad started it. He drove out to the street. The cab was already a block away. Brad sped after it. He kept two cars in between. Then Bea Jones wouldn't know she was being tailed.

The cab went on for many blocks. Then it slowed down and stopped at the curb. Brad drove past it. He parked in the next block. They jumped out.

"Bea's going in a tailor shop," Meg said.

Brad spotted a cafe across the street. There were two tables outside.

He and Meg rushed over and sat at one. Their view was good. They could see inside the shop. Bea talked to a man. She took out an envelope and showed him something.

Brad pulled up his camera for a better look. "It's the pictures," he told Meg.

A waiter came out of the cafe. He handed them menus. Brad tried to look at it and watch the shop, too. He ordered something. Meg did, too. The waiter went back in.

"Now the woman is coming out. She must be leaving," Meg said.

The woman walked out to the cab. But she didn't get in. Al got out. He went back inside with her.

*Brad and Meg rushed over
and sat down at an outside table.*

24

Now the man pulled out his tape. He began measuring Al.

Brad looked at Meg. "This doesn't make sense," he said.

The waiter brought out their food. Brad ate with his eyes on the tailor shop. At last the tailor was done.

Brad left money on the table. Then he and Meg dashed back to his car. They watched Bea and Al come out.

"Where is she going next?" Meg asked.

Al started the cab. He turned and drove back down the street. Brad went after him. He drove straight to Bea's apartment. She got out and went into the building.

Al swung the cab around and parked in front of Carl's. He got out and went in.

"Let's go talk to him," Meg said.

"O.K., but let's talk to the tailor first," Brad said.

They drove back down the street. There was a parking spot in front of the tailor's shop.

The tailor frowned when they came in. "I'll be glad to help you. But don't ask for anything in a hurry. I don't have time. Today a woman showed me pictures. She wanted a suit just like them for her limo driver. It has to be done by Friday morning," he said.

Brad looked at the pictures on the table. They were of Casper Lloyd's driver.

CHAPTER 5

Calling the Police

Brad and Meg rushed back to Carl's. Al was still inside. So was Walt Conner.

Carl smiled as they walked in. "Coffee?" he asked.

Brad nodded. Then he turned to Al. "I saw a goodlooking woman get out of your cab. Do you know her name?" he asked.

Al shook his head. "No, but I got a good fare. The woman wanted to go to a store. She asked me to wait while she shopped," he said.

Brad glanced at Meg. And she looked at him. Both of them knew he was lying.

Walt Conner spoke up. "Your story about Denton Bay was in the morning news. I liked it," he said.

Carl brought over the coffee. "You should do a story on Casper Lloyd. He's as interesting as Denton Bay and a lot richer. That man must have a clock in his brain. He is always on time. It happens each day. His limo drives in at 10 o'clock. The driver waits until noon. He takes Casper Lloyd to lunch. They come back at 1 o'clock. Then the driver leaves. He comes back at 5 o'clock. Casper Lloyd walks out of the bank and they go home," he said.

Meg smiled. "A story about the banker is a good idea," she said.

Brad sipped his coffee. But thoughts kept bothering him. Why did Bea Jones want the suit by Friday? And why did Al lie?

Meg must have been thinking the same thoughts. She stood up. "Come on. We've got work to do," she told Brad.

They went back to the newsroom. Bea sat at her window. But she wasn't looking through the binoculars. They were on the table near her.

"I don't think she's from the police. Why would they want pictures of a limo driver?" Meg asked.

"I agree. It's no police stakeout. That's

what worries me. Maybe it's a plot to rob the bank," Brad said.

"I thought of that, too," Meg said.

Once again Brad dialed the police. Sergeant Ward wasn't back. So he talked to Officer Niles.

The officer listened to Brad's story. "No, we don't have a stakeout there. We'll check this. I'll get back to you," he said.

Brad and Meg acted as if they were working. But they watched out the window. Bea was still sitting in the window.

A police car came up the street. It parked in front of the apartment. Two officers got out and went inside.

"One of them is Officer Niles. They're

going up to talk to Bea now," Brad said.

"She just left the window. So they must be knocking on her door," Meg said.

They kept watching. An hour went by. At last the policemen came out. One of them walked over to Carl's. He and Al came out. They talked for a few minutes. Then Al went back in Carl's. And the policeman walked to the door of the News.

"He's coming up here," Meg said.

The officer came in the newsroom. He walked to their desks. "You're Brad Jones and Meg Green. Aren't you?" he asked.

"That's right," Brad said.

"I'm Officer Niles. Thank you for the call.

It could have been a plot against the bank. But it isn't. Bea Jones took pictures of Casper Lloyd's driver. She wants a suit like his. It's for her brother. His birthday is Friday. He's a limo driver in Brighton. I called and checked her story," he said.

"Why did Al lie?" Brad asked.

"He felt silly about being measured," the officer said.

It was 5 o'clock when the man left. Brad glanced outside. The black limo had pulled up to the bank. Casper Lloyd came out. Brad looked at the window. The woman watched through her binoculars.

CHAPTER 6

Getting the Facts

Brad turned to Meg. "Why does she watch the bank and Casper Lloyd now? I don't believe her story," he said.

"Neither do I. Officer Niles checked it out too fast. I think Bea and Al are both new in town. I haven't seen them before," she said.

Brad nodded. "Bea watches the bank. Al hangs out in Carl's. That's next door. They're planning something on Friday. It has to do with Casper Lloyd's driver," he said.

"I'll check them out tomorrow," Meg said.

Brad stopped at the apartment house the next morning. He wanted to see what Bea was watching. The fourth floor hall had a good view. He could see the bank lobby. Casper Lloyd's office was on the floor above. Brad could even see the clock on his desk.

Al and Walt Conner were in Carl's. So Brad stopped in. He might learn more about Al.

Walt raved about Denton Bay. He had been to the play last night. "You should have seen the crowd waiting to see him come out," he said.

Carl frowned. "That means the crowds will be here Friday afternoon, too. Riddle Street will be a mess," he said.

"I went back to Denton Bay's dressing room. He talked to me," Walt bragged.

Carl laughed. "Watch out. You'll start to act like him," he said.

Brad turned to Al. "How do you like Star City. You're new here. Aren't you?" he asked.

"No, I've just been working on the other side of town," Al told him.

Brad left and went back to the newsroom. He told Meg about Al. "He's from the other side of town," he said.

Meg shook her head. "His full name is Al Jones. He is Bea's brother. They're both from Brighton. Yes, he did drive a limo. But he quit one week ago," she said.

Brad frowned. "Al quit driving a limo so he could drive a cab. That doesn't make sense. What about Bea?" he asked.

"Bea Jones worked in a camera store. She quit a week ago and moved here. She drives a gray car," she said.

"Why did she move here?" Brad asked.

"Bea said she was joining her boyfriend," Meg told him.

"So there's another man in the plot. I wonder who he is," Brad said.

"And I called Casper Lloyd. I have a meeting with him on Friday," Meg added.

Brad smiled. "Good! You'll be in the bank. We need to watch it on Friday," he said.

CHAPTER 7

The Kidnapping

Friday morning came. But nothing happened. Now it was Friday afternoon. The crowd formed on Riddle Street. Denton Bay's play was almost over. They waited for him to come out.

Brad and Meg were down on the street, too. But he watched the bank as he took pictures.

"What time is it?" Meg asked.

"It's 4:10," Brad told her.

"My meeting with Casper Lloyd is at 4:15," Meg said. She walked to the bank.

Brad snapped pictures. Only a few minutes went by. Then he saw Meg coming back.

"Your watch is slow. I missed my meeting. Casper Lloyd's clock said 4:45 when I walked in. So we set up another time," she told him.

"My watch isn't slow," Brad said.

"Yes, it is. Here comes the black limo now," Meg said.

Brad had his camera in his hand. He looked through it. "That's not his driver. It looks like Al. That's not Casper Lloyd's limo either. It's not shiny enough," Brad told her.

"Denton Bay is coming out of the Palace. But he's not going to his limo. He's headed for Carl's. The crowd is following," Meg said.

"Something's wrong! Wait here! I'll get my car. We'll follow that limo," Brad said.

Brad raced to his car. The limo was gone when he got back.

Meg jumped in and pointed down the street. "They went that way. Casper Lloyd didn't get a good look at his limo or the driver. The crowd was too thick. The limo roared off as soon as he got inside. I think he was kidnapped," she said.

Brad nodded. He roared down the road, too. Now the limo came into view. It was a block ahead.

Meg grabbed Brad's car phone. She called the police.

Meg grabbed Brad's car phone.

"This is Sergeant Ward," came a voice.

"Oh, Sergeant Ward, I'm glad to hear you. Brad and I are following a black limo. We think Casper Lloyd has been kidnapped," Meg said.

"Where are you?" Sergeant Ward asked.

"We've just turned off Riddle Street. Now we're on Front Street," Meg told him.

"Be careful. We're on our way," Sergeant Ward said.

This was an old part of town. The road got rough. Warehouses were on both sides. The limo slowed down and turned in one of them.

Brad slammed on his brakes and parked a half block away. "This must be their hideout. They'll wait here for the ransom money," he said.

Soon police cars roared up behind them. Sergeant Ward jumped out and ran to their car.

"I'm glad you're safe. You're right. We've had reports that Casper Lloyd was kidnapped. His real driver and limo are at the bank now," Sergeant Ward said.

"Denton Bay might be in on the plot. I saw him walk down the street to Carl's. That's what caused the crowd in front of the bank. Casper Lloyd couldn't see that it wasn't his limo or his driver," Meg told him.

"We've had reports on that, too. Denton Bay is still in the Palace. Someone stole his hat and coat," Sergeant Ward said.

"A man dressed like Bay. He raced through

Carl's Coffee Shop. A gray car was waiting for him out back," Sergeant Ward went on.

"That was Bea's car. But who was the man?" Brad asked.

The police circled the warehouse. Then Sergeant Ward got on the loud speaker. "Come out. Or we will shoot," he ordered.

The doors opened. Out came Al, Bea, Casper Lloyd, and a tall man.

"It's Walt Conner! He's Bea's boyfriend!" Meg gasped.

"That's why Walt had tickets to so many plays. He went backstage. That's where Denton Bay's hat and coat were," Brad said.

Casper Lloyd rushed toward them. "Thank

you for saving me, Sergeant Ward," he said.

"Thank Brad and Meg. They're the ones who solved this case," Sergeant Ward said.

"There's just one thing we can't figure out. Why was your clock fast?" Brad asked.

Casper Lloyd pointed to Walt. "That man came to see me this afternoon. He asked me to check some facts. I went to my files. He must have set my clock ahead then," he said.

"It almost worked," Walt growled.

Casper Lloyd turned to Brad and Meg. "How can I thank you?" he asked.

Brad grinned. "Just give us a story," he told him.